THE BIG COWHUNA

written and illustrated by

MIKE LITWIN

ALBERT WHITMAN & COMPANY
CHICAGO, ILLINOIS

for Kelly

Library of Congress Cataloging-in-Publication data is on file with the publisher.

Text and illustrations copyright © 2015 Mike Litwin
Published in 2015 by Albert Whitman & Company
ISBN 978-0-8075-8720-1
Printed in China.
10 9 8 7 6 5 4 3 2 1 NP 20 19 18 17 16 15 14

For more information about Albert Whitman & Company,
visit our web site at www.albertwhitman.com.

CONTENTS

THE PEACEFUL DAY

For hundreds of years, the secret, sunny island of Bermooda was a rather uneventful place. There were plenty of exciting and enjoyable moments, of course, but always in the name of progress or good fun. It was rare that the cows of Bermooda saw anything dangerous or out of the ordinary happen. Most things on this tiny tropical paradise were just as peaceful

1

and predictable as the constant rolling of ocean waves upon the shore. But that was all before the days of Chuck and Dakota Porter.

Sure, lots of folks have talents. Some folks have a knack for swimming and sailing, some have a knack for baking coconut cheesecake, and some even have a knack for growing beautiful hibiscus flowers. In the case of Chuck and Dakota Porter…well, they had a knack for finding trouble, even in a place like Bermooda.

It had all started the day Chuck found Dakota washed up on a sandbar. Dakota was not a cow like Chuck. Nor was he a pig, a bird, a monkey, or any of the other animals that walked, talked, and lived on the island.

Dakota was a hu'man, a savage creature everyone believed had been extinct for ages. No one on the island had ever seen a hu'man before, and no one seemed to know much about them, except for the legend about how they were nothing but monsters that ate cows and breathed fire. To keep the island from plunging into panic, Chuck dressed Dakota in "cowmouflage"—a cow costume to hide his real identity. Since Dakota had no home and no family, Chuck brought him home to the Porter House. Dakota was eventually adopted into the family, though no one had any clue he was really a hu'man.

Ever since then, life on Bermooda had become much more eventful. Chuck was a daring calf, and if he couldn't find any excitement, he'd simply make some. This bold spirit constantly led him and his newly adopted brother into dangerous and thrilling situations. It seemed like every day was a new adventure.

Today, however, was not one of those days. Today was quiet and peaceful. No mysteries, no discoveries, no adventures of any kind. Just the crashing of waves, a warm breeze, and the gentle cawing of seagulls. As far as Dakota was concerned, it was the perfect way to spend a Saturday. Dakota was far less interested in adventure or excitement than Chuck. He would much rather spend the day lying in the thick grass under the tall trees, wearing a straw hat and filling up on delicious bananas. That is what they were doing on this Saturday in particular.

"Pass me another banana," Dakota said.

"This is the last one," Chuck said, tossing it to him. "If you want more, you'll have to climb another tree."

Dakota looked up at the trees towering over them. Bermooda's banana trees stood nearly twenty feet tall. Clumps of yummy yellow bananas teased their eyes, dangling up out of reach. Bermooda's cows were capable of doing many things that an average cow could not, but climbing trees was not one of them.

However, Dakota was excellent at climbing trees since he had fingers and toes instead of hooves. His climbing was not quite as fast as

a monkey's, but it saved them the trouble of dragging out a ladder. But Dakota felt quite relaxed at the moment and was not in the mood to scramble back up and fetch any more bananas. Propping his back against a tree, he pulled his straw hat down over his eyes and folded his hands behind his head.

Meanwhile Chuck paced back and forth in the grass. "I'm soooooo boooooored!" he mooed. "Aren't you bored?"

"Nope," Dakota replied from under his hat.

"Doesn't it feel like something should happen?" Chuck asked.

"Nope," Dakota repeated.

"Don't you want to do anything exciting?" Chuck whined.

"Nope," Dakota sighed. "I'm just fine right here."

Dakota heard the sound of Chuck clomping over to him. Suddenly his eyes were treated to a flood of warm sunlight as Chuck pulled the hat off his face.

"Can we at least take a walk?" Chuck asked.

Dakota blinked in the sudden brightness. "Sure," he said, adjusting his cow mask as he climbed to his feet.

They ambled toward the beach and then strolled along the shore, with Dakota eating his last banana and Chuck complaining about his boredom all the way.

"I wish something amazing would happen," he mumbled, picking up a rock from the beach. "We've probably made this boring walk a billion times." He pitched the rock far ahead of them. It whizzed through the air and landed in the soft sand with a loud *clank!*

Chuck and Dakota exchanged confused looks.

"What was that clanking noise?" Chuck wondered aloud.

They trotted up to the place where the rock had landed, looking for the source of the sound. There, half-buried in the sand, they found a shiny purple shell.

Chuck was immediately fascinated. He had always been interested in shells, and he had become a bit of an expert. Not only did he learn about them in school, but he also took extra time on his own to research the ones displayed in the Hortica Center, the island's museum. But of all the shells he had studied, he had never seen one like this.

The shell was twisted into a cone-shaped spiral like a tiny tornado. But the shell's shape wasn't what made it so bizarre. Its

entire surface was covered with a pattern of loops and swirls, as if thousands of permanent fingerprints had been left all over it. A string of symbols was etched along its twisted spiral curve. They almost looked like letters but not in any language that Chuck or Dakota could read.

"Wow!" Chuck said as his tail twitched all over the place. "Now *this* is amazing!" He turned the shell over in his hooves. "Look at these weird loopy patterns! And these markings! It almost looks like some kind of ancient writing. I've never seen anything like this before."

"Well, I guess there's a first time for everything," Dakota said with a shrug.

▐▌

"No, you don't get it," Chuck said, shaking his head. "This is impossible. Nothing like this occurs in nature. *This shell shouldn't be here.*"

They looked down at the strange shell. Glowing in the slanted light of the late afternoon sun, it almost looked alive. A gleam ran across its pearly purple surface, as if it were telling them it was happy to be found.

"Are you going to keep it?" Dakota asked.

"Of course," Chuck said. "You know I like to collect cool stuff."

Dakota looked at the excited expression on Chuck's face. He suddenly had a feeling things were about to become a lot less peaceful.

THE IMPOSSIBLE

Chuck held the shell up to his ear. "Wow! I can hear the ocean!"

"*Of course* you can hear the ocean," Dakota answered, rolling his eyes. "It's only twenty feet away."

Chuck ignored the comment. Dakota was never easily amazed, and Chuck wasn't going to let him ruin his excitement. "I have an idea!

13

We should take it to the Hortica Center!" he suggested. "Maybe Cornelius knows what kind of shell it is."

Cornelius was the screech owl who ran the island's museum. To the best of everyone's knowledge, he was the expert on all things related to Bermooda's history, residents, and environment. If anyone could tell them about this shell, it would be him.

The Hortica Center was across the island in the middle of Bermooda Village. By the time Chuck and Dakota walked over there, the sun was already sitting low in the deep orange sky. They arrived to find Cornelius fluttering with his back to them, closing the museum doors for the evening.

"Wait!" Chuck mooed, hoofing it up to the doors. "Cornelius, wait!"

The sound of Chuck's voice surprised Cornelius. It was unusual for calves to visit the museum so close to suppertime on a Saturday, even a calf as curious as Chuck. The little owl jumped with a start and several brown feathers molted from his back, fluttering to the ground as he turned.

"Good evening, Mister Porter," Cornelius said in his cultured, proper voice. "And the *other* Mister Porter," he nodded his head at Dakota. "Shouldn't you two be at home having supper?"

"We found something we wanted you to look at," Chuck said, catching his breath. He held up the glittery purple shell for Cornelius to see.

"Oh, now…that *is* interesting," Cornelius hooted. "Very interesting indeed." He opened the museum doors with his feet. "Bring that inside and we'll take a closer look."

Chuck and Dakota followed Cornelius into the main hall of the museum, where they stopped at the front desk. Behind the desk, Cornelius landed on a bamboo perch underneath a brass sign that read: *H.M.S. Hortica.* This was where Cornelius sat to greet visitors whenever he wasn't giving an official tour. Chuck put the shell on the desk for Cornelius to examine. As the two of them inspected the new discovery, Dakota looked at the exhibits around them.

The museum was a fascinating place. It displayed all kinds of relics from the *H.M.S. Hortica*—the hu'man ship full of cows that had wrecked on Bermooda hundreds of years ago. There were globes, spyglasses, books, and clothing. It was the only real connection Dakota—or anyone—had with the lost hu'man world.

Cornelius squinted at the shell through the gold-rimmed monocle over his left eye, and then he hooted the same line Chuck had uttered on the beach.

"I've never seen anything like this before," he said. "Not in nature, nor in history. None that *I've* studied anyway. This is... impossible." He stared blankly at the shell for a moment, and then he flapped down from his perch and rummaged around a small bookshelf in a dark corner behind the desk. He carried back a thick volume with pages that shone with pale gold edges. Little clouds of dust flew up from the book as it landed on the desk with a thud. Pressed into its dingy green cover was the title *Compendium of the Impossible.*

"Com-pen-dee-um?" Dakota sounded out the word. "What does that mean?"

"A compendium is a reference book," Cornelius explained. "This one contains accounts of impossible objects from history, written by ancient hu'mans who claimed to have seen them."

"'Claimed' to have seen?" Chuck asked. "They didn't *actually* see them?"

"It's difficult to tell," Cornelius muttered almost in a whisper. "These were fabled trinkets that no one had seen before and no one has seen since. Hu'mans said these objects were capable of mysterious and terrible magic!"

"Magic?" Dakota said, his voice trembling slightly.

"Only if you believe in that sort of thing," Cornelius said. "I'm sure there was nothing really special about those items. But perhaps your shell has been seen before."

Chuck and Dakota leafed through the wrinkly pages. Most of the museum's books were about science, art, history, and sailing, but none of them were as interesting as this one. It was filled with illustrations of mystical objects: a flying carpet, a glowing trident, a smoking mirror…the pictures went on page after page. However, they saw nothing that looked like the twisted purple shell in front of them. If the shell was in the book, it could take hours—even days—for them to find it.

Chuck looked around at all the books on their display stands. "Hey, Cornelius, why isn't this book on display with the others?"

"This is not a book of facts or culture," Cornelius explained. "This is a book of lore. Legends. Stories. Fairy tales. This book is certainly wonderful for the imagination, but it should only be read for entertainment, not education." He polished his monocle with a feather before putting it back over his eye. "There is no magic, Mister Porter. That's why these objects are called impossible."

Chuck and Dakota fixed their eyes on a page that showed a giant crab guarding a familiar-looking coral crown with rays of light coming from it. Cornelius didn't know that they had actually seen this magical object before. But Chuck and Dakota knew they would never convince him it was real.

"Though I must admit it is quite an odd little thing," Cornelius continued as he gazed at the gleaming shell. "It's almost as though that shell doesn't belong here."

As soon as those words escaped his beak, Cornelius wished he could take them back. Cornelius—like most everyone on the island— believed that nothing of importance existed outside of Bermooda. He didn't want to feed any of Chuck's fantasies about great big worlds beyond the horizon.

"Even so, there must be some natural explanation," he hooted with a harrumph, adjusting his monocle. "Mister Porter, I wonder if you'd let us hold on to that shell here at the museum. It's a very rare find, and we'd love to have it as part of our collection."

Dakota could see that Cornelius was very interested in the shell, almost as interested as Chuck was.

"Sorry, Cornelius," Chuck said. "I kind of have my own collection of rare finds, and it would be awfully incomplete without this. Thanks for your help though. *Moohalo.*"

Chuck and Dakota exited the Hortica Center and started off for home.

"Why are you keeping that thing?" Dakota asked. "Why don't you just leave it at the museum?" He was getting more creeped out by this shell every minute, ever since Cornelius mentioned the word "magic."

"Cornelius knows pretty much everything, and even *he* can't tell what this is," Chuck said. "So any trinket that's weird enough to stump him is weird enough to go in my collection."

3

WEiRD THiNGS

Cornelius may not have been much help with the shell, but he had been right about one thing: Chuck and Dakota *were* supposed to be home having supper. They got home late, and everyone at the Porters' long supper table looked up at them when they finally arrived halfway through the meal.

Suppertime was a big deal at the Porter

House. The house had many extra rooms that Mama and Papa Porter rented out for folks to live in, so their dinner table always had lots of friends and family. Some of them came to the Porter House for only a short while, but there were some who stayed for years.

There were Mama and Papa Porter, of course, along with Chuck's know-it-all little sister, Patty, and his rowdy Uncle Bo. There was also Miss Magnolia, the prim-and-proper heifer; Quincy, the cranky old hedgehog; and Ditto, the loud, squawky parrot, among many others. Chuck and Dakota made their apologies for being late, sat down at the long table, and got to eating. Chuck piled his plate high with Bermooda grass. Dakota carefully chewed on a mouthful of carrots under his cowmouflage mask.

Dakota didn't really like wearing his cowmouflage. He was certainly grateful to have something that allowed him to roam among the cows and call Bermooda his home, but he still hated having to put it on.

For one thing, it was ugly. Chuck had thrown the whole thing together with the objects he had on-hoof when he found Dakota: an old brown blanket, a piece of sponge, a couple of whale's teeth, and some coconut shells. The whole thing was crudely stitched together with vines and twine. The only thing more amazing than how quickly Chuck made the disguise was the fact that no one seemed to realize the dreadful thing was just a costume.

Not only did the cowmouflage look awful, it felt awful too. The blanket that covered Dakota's body was often hot and itchy. The spongy cow nose that masked his face made it hard to see sometimes. And the coconut hooves that covered his hands made him feel very clumsy.

It wasn't just that the cowmouflage was ugly and uncomfortable though. More than that, Dakota really just hated that he had to wear a disguise at all. The Porters were his family now—they were his *kine*—and he hated having to lie to them. At least three times a week he felt the urge to tear off his cow mask and loudly cry, "Look! See? I'm a hu'man! I'm not a monster! I don't breathe fire or have long, sharp claws! And I'm not going to eat you!" But Chuck insisted that something like that would throw the entire family—and the entire *island*—into a panic. Hu'mans were supposed to be extinct. Dakota couldn't help but think that everything would be so much easier if he were just a real cow.

"Are you two ready to watch the big surf contest tomorrow?" Papa Porter asked.

"You bet!" Chuck cheered. "Wahu Brahman is going to kick tail!"

Tomorrow would be the Cowabunga Classic, a big surf competition held once a year. Lots of surfcows would be competing, but

Wahu Brahman was the heavy favorite to win. In fact, Wahu was always the heavy favorite. He had won the last seven years in a row.

"You know, I bet I get to be as good a surfer as Wahu Brahman someday," Chuck said.

Ditto screeched out a squawky laugh.

Quincy nearly choked on his bite of corn muffin.

Patty spat out the words, "Are you *kidding*?"

Their reaction was understandable. Chuck had tried surfing three times in his life. The first time, he spent four hours just trying to stand up on the board. The second time, he tumbled off and landed face-first in a school of jellyfish. The third time, he got tossed by a wave that broke the board completely in half.

"First ya gotta learn to stand up there, Chucky!" Uncle Bo laughed, his big belly shaking. "How ya gonna do that with only half a board?"

"That's not at all polite, Bo," Miss Magnolia said curtly. "Everyone makes mistakes."

"I believe it will take a lot of practice, dear," Mama Porter said. "But I'm sure you can do it, if that's what you wish."

"You wish! You wish!" Ditto cawed.

After dinner, Chuck and Dakota retreated to their room, where Dakota peeled out of his cowmouflage almost immediately.

Chuck reviewed his Collection of Weird Things displayed in a wooden tray on his clothes dresser. Above the dresser, a poster of Wahu Brahman hung on the wall. Posing heroically, the big blue bull held a surfboard with the word *Brahman* branded into it. Proudly blazoned across the bottom of the poster were the words, *The Big Cowhuna.*

The trinkets in Chuck's collection were nowhere near as impressive as the ones in Cornelius's book. Chuck was disappointed that the most interesting trinkets—the stuff he and Dakota had found on their adventures— were missing from the set. Monstrous costumes, magic hornpipes, coral crowns… those things always seemed to get lost, broken, or claimed by their rightful owners. This impossible purple shell would definitely be the "Big Cowhuna" of his collection.

Chuck put the shell up to his ear again. "Listen! I can still hear the ocean!"

Dakota folded his arms. "It's not really the ocean, you know," he said with his eyes closed. "It's air echoing inside the empty shell. Everyone knows that. It just *sounds* like the ocean."

"Oh yeah?" Chuck said. "Complete with seagulls and everything?"

Dakota's eyes fluttered open. "What? Give me that," he said, taking the shell from Chuck's hooves. He held it up to his ear. Sure enough, he heard more than just the dull roar of air in an empty shell. He heard loud crashing waves, gusts of wind, and the familiar cawing of seagulls. He could even smell the salty spray of the sea.

Dakota pulled the shell away from his face. "That's...that's impossible," he stammered.

"No, it's incredible!" Chuck said firmly. "It's kind of like the shell is alive."

The hair on Dakota's neck stood up. He too had felt like the shell was alive when Chuck first picked it up off the beach. But the very idea seemed so silly that he wasn't about to admit it.

"Oh, sure. It's alive," Dakota joked, rolling his eyes. He knocked on the shell three times and shouted into the open end. "Helloooooo in theeeeerrre!"

They instantly felt a breeze flow through the room. Normally, this would not be surprising. Bermooda was often a breezy place. But this time, the grass curtains covering their windows blew *out*, not *in*. The breeze was coming from *inside the shell*.

The sounds of the ocean grew louder to the point that Dakota half-expected waves to come pouring in through the windows. Out of the shell hissed a purple cloud that twisted itself into a cyclone shape, much like the shape of the shell itself. It spun in the middle of their bedroom like a whirlwind in slow motion. Chuck and Dakota dove for cover, not sure what to expect. Suddenly waves and seagulls were not the only sounds they heard. From inside the cloud, a voice spoke: "I… am…ZEPHYR."

ZEPHYR

"What is that thing?" Dakota screeched.

"I am Zephyr," the whirlwind repeated. "I am your servant, sirs." Its voice was calm and soothing, just like waves on the beach.

"The tornado can talk!" Chuck said.

"Zeff-er?" Dakota pronounced the name slowly. "What do you want?"

Some of the swirling clouds twisted into

eyes and a mouth, giving the tornado a bit of a face. Each time it spoke, a bright warm light glowed inside as if this cyclone had swallowed the sun itself.

"As I said, I am your servant," the talking tornado replied. "So I am here to serve you, sirs."

Chuck's eyes darted back and forth. "Serve us what?" he asked.

"Whatever you wish," Zephyr said.

Whatever we wish? Dakota thought to himself. *That's impossible!* Then his mind wandered back to the book they'd looked at in the Hortica Center—the book of impossible objects. The objects that ancient hu'mans claimed were magic.

"Wait. Are you…a *genie*?" Dakota asked.

"What's a genie?" Chuck whispered, a little embarrassed by his ignorance.

"A genie is a thing that lives in a magic lamp or a bottle," Dakota explained. "There was a picture of one in Cornelius's book. When you call the genie out, it grants you three wishes!"

"*Three* wishes?" Zephyr echoed. "Why, I could never imagine myself being so selfish. There are no limitations on wishes, sir. As long as you hold my shell, I shall be happy to grant any wish you ask with no limits."

Chuck and Dakota looked at each other with their jaws hanging wide open. "Unlimited wishes!" they both gasped.

"As many as you can think of, sirs." Zephyr beamed. "I've been making dreams come true for thousands of years."

"We could have whatever we want!" Chuck said. "What should we wish for?"

Dakota thought for a moment. What should his first wish be? "Okay, Zephyr," he finally said, "I wish for…bananas!"

Chuck looked at Dakota in disbelief. "Bananas?" he asked. Was that all Dakota could think to wish for? Hu'mans certainly didn't have much imagination.

"That's right," Dakota continued. "Enough bananas that I never have to climb a banana tree again!"

"Oh! Not just *any* bananas," Chuck chimed

in, putting his hooves on the shell. "We wish for chocolate-covered bananas! *Tons* of them!"

"As you wish," Zephyr agreed. With that, he began to spin faster and faster.

The sound of the ocean rose once again as the breeze in the room began to whip and whirl. As their hair blew in the wind, Chuck and Dakota heard little popping noises all around them. When the wind died down, they found themselves surrounded by piles and piles of bananas all over the bedroom.

"Whoa!" Chuck said, his jaw hanging open once again. "Magic bananas!"

Dakota studied the massive piles. They looked like ordinary bananas to him— besides the fact that they had appeared out of thin air, of course. He picked up one of the bananas and peeled it. Underneath the peel, he found that the entire banana was coated in chocolate.

"Looks like chocolate to me," Chuck said. He took a banana for himself and peeled it. The chocolate part was his idea after all, and he couldn't wait to try one. "Tastes like chocolate too," he said, taking a bite.

"If you'll not be needing me for now, sirs, I shall return to my shell," Zephyr said. "Please enjoy yourselves."

Dakota peeked past Zephyr into the shell's opening. "It sounded like there was a whole beach in your shell," he said. "Doesn't it get cramped in there?"

"Oh, no, sir," the windy genie said. "It is quite comfortable. And peaceful too." Zephyr sounded very polite, like a butler. He also didn't seem surprised at all by the fact that Dakota was a hu'man. It was like he'd seen hu'mans plenty of times before. As the genie disappeared back into his shell, Dakota suspected Zephyr had seen so many things that nothing could surprise him.

Chuck and Dakota quickly finished their bananas then grabbed two more. It was the sweetest chocolate they could remember ever tasting. They wolfed the bananas down almost immediately, then grabbed even more.

It went that way for hours: peel a banana, gobble it down, then grab another…and another…and another. In fact, the more they ate, the more bananas there seemed to be. It was like they could never run out. They could eat chocolate-covered bananas all through the night until their sides split open, without ever having to climb a tree again.

They were magic bananas indeed.

5

A Real Change

Dakota woke up the next morning feeling like someone had driven a banana cart over his stomach. *How many bananas did we eat last night?* he wondered. He had lost count after two dozen or so. All he could remember was eating and eating and eating. The floor was littered with empty peels from their unlimited supply of treats.

"Uuuggghhhhhh…" he heard from the other side of the room. Chuck was waking up. Rubbing his eyes, he emerged from underneath a pile of banana peels.

"Does your stomach hurt as much as mine?" Dakota groaned.

"Yeah," Chuck moaned back, *all four* of my stomachs. Was it because of all the bananas?" Chuck's ability to eat was almost as big as his appetite, so he was not used to feeling to sick after a huge meal.

"Maybe the chocolate idea was a bit much," Dakota suggested, frowning at an empty banana peel.

Chuck rolled on his back and stared at the ceiling. Even with the rumbly ache he felt inside, every one of their chocolate-covered goodies had been delicious. "It was worth it," he sighed.

They had both slept so late that they'd missed breakfast. In fact, it was already nearing noon. The Cowabunga Classic would start in a few hours. Missing breakfast didn't bother them though, since they were both feeling so bad in the belly.

"Now aren't you glad I didn't donate this shell to the museum?" Chuck bragged, picking up the shell from under a banana peel.

Dakota hated to admit it, but he *was* kind of glad, even with his stomach so sick.

"What should we wish for next?" Chuck asked as Dakota put on his hot, uncomfortable cowmouflage.

"I don't know," Dakota said. He slipped the coconut-shell hooves over his hands like an awkward pair of gloves. "Maybe we should wish for someone to clean up all these banana peels."

"No, no. Think bigger than that," Chuck said. "We have an awesome power here in our hooves!"

Dakota snorted out a laugh. *In our hooves?* He didn't have hooves. All he had was a pair of clunky, clumsy coconut gloves that covered his real hands.

"Okay…we should wish for someone to clean up *all of our messes*," Dakota suggested, putting on his fake cow nose. "From now until the day we die." He could feel his warm breath against the spongy mask as he slid it over his face.

"That would be a lot of messes," Chuck admitted. "But no. No, no, no. A *lot* bigger. We could have anything we want! Think of something that could make a real change."

Dakota pulled against the itchy collar rubbing against his neck. One of the stitches popped open on his coconut-clad hand, stinging his shoulder. His face flushed hot with anger. He'd had enough of this cowmouflage.

"Anything I want? Fine!" he shouted, taking the shell from Chuck. "I'll show you a real change." He rapped three times on the shell. *Clang! Clang! Clang!* "Helloooooo in there!"

Once again, a refreshing breeze circled them as a familiar purple cloud twisted out of the shell. Waves rumbled. Curtains blew. Banana peels skittered to the edges of the room.

"Good morning, sir," Zephyr said, polite as always. "Ah, I see you've made a charming cow costume since I've been away. That's very 'a-moo-sing,' sir."

"It's not amusing," Dakota said. "It's annoying. But you're going to change that right now, Swirly."

"Do you wish me to give you a different costume, sir?" Zephyr asked calmly.

"A bigger change than that," Dakota said. "Zephyr...I wish to be...*a real cow*."

Zephyr didn't respond right away. For a moment, Dakota thought maybe he had wished *too* big. But after a short pause came Zephyr's line: "As you wish."

The wind swirled around the room in gusts as Zephyr spun faster and faster, just like the night before. Banana peels flew everywhere.

I sure hope this works, Dakota thought. He closed his eyes to avoid getting a flying banana peel stuck to them.

Once the wind calmed down and banana peels were no longer flinging about, Dakota cracked open his eyelids. At first, he didn't feel any different. Then he noticed that he was terribly hot—even hotter than usual in his cowmouflage. He soon realized that his mask was pushed so far away that he could see the back of it without having to cross his eyes. It was no longer sitting on his face. It was resting on the edge of a long cow nose!

He reached up to pull off the mask and found that the coconut shells he wore over his hands had broken off and fallen to the floor. He now had a pair of real hooves. Forgetting all about his stomachache, Dakota shook with excitement as he ripped off his cowmouflage. Underneath, he found that he was covered with thick brown hair from horns to hoof.

"No wonder I was so much hotter in that costume!" he squealed happily. He stared at himself in the mirror. He looked almost exactly like Chuck, except that he was brown like the blanket from his cowmouflage.

Dakota reached up to the top of his shaggy head. Two tiny little horns now stuck up from the moppy hair that still covered his noggin. They didn't wiggle like the ones on his costume. When he pulled on these horns, he was pulling his head too.

"This is incredible!" he cried. "Look! Real horns! And real hair! See?"

Chuck could hardly believe his eyes. Without thinking much about it, he reached behind Dakota and tugged his tail.

"Ow!" Dakota said.

"Sorry," Chuck said. "Just checking."

"Don't be sorry! I have a tail!" Dakota cheered. "*I have a tail!*"

"I hope you're pleased, sir," Zephyr said.

But Dakota didn't even hear the genie. He was too excited. He'd finally be able to hug Mama Porter without worrying about his mask coming off. Or give Papa a high-hoof without worrying about cracking a coconut shell. Without so much as a *"Moohalo,"* he and Chuck scampered off downstairs, leaving Zephyr among the banana peels.

"I hope it's everything you wished for, sir," Zephyr called from the bedroom as the door slammed shut. "Everything…and more."

Chuck and Dakota bounded into the Porters' big sitting room. They stood next to each other, looking almost like twins. Papa was reading the moospaper while chewing on a long stalk of beach grass. Uncle Bo was eating, as usual—gobbling down cornbread and dropping crumbs all over himself.

Mama looked up from her chair, where she was stitching up a seam in Patty's dress as Patty did her best to stand still. "Good afternoon, Chuck," she greeted him. "Who's your new friend?"

Chuck and Dakota wrinkled their matching noses in confusion. Was that a joke? Mama certainly didn't appear to be joking. She looked as if she didn't recognize Dakota at all.

"Where's Dakota?" Papa Porter asked. "You both missed breakfast this morning. We assumed you headed out to the beach early."

Everyone in the room looked blankly at them, waiting for an answer. A few silent moments went by before Chuck and Dakota finally realized: *No one had any idea that the cow in front of them was Dakota.*

SHELDON

Everyone stared as Chuck and Dakota stood in shock, searching for an answer. Neither of them knew what to say. Normally, Dakota would start to sweat nervously at a time like this. But he was a real cow now, and cows didn't sweat. Chuck thought only of their magic shell. What had they done?

"This is…um…shell…done. Yeah—*Sheldon*,"

Chuck stuttered. "He lives…ummm…on the southern part of the island. Near the Boneyard."

"The Boneyard?" Uncle Bo repeated with a sloppy burp. "Well, tan my hide! I didn't think anyone lived near the Boneyard."

The Boneyard was the shipwrecked remains of the *H.M.S. Hortica*. It was nothing but a bunch of old timbers sticking out of the ground, but island legend said that it was haunted, and few cows dared to go there.

"I've never seen you before," Patty said, cocking her head and squinting. She was only six, but she was quite sharp. "Why haven't I seen you at school?"

Dakota had heard this question before. Patty had asked the very same thing the day Chuck brought Dakota home in cowmouflage.

"Be polite, Patty," Mama gently scolded, continuing to stitch her dress. "And stop fidgeting."

"It's because he sits in the *back* of the room with me, squirt," Chuck said. "Little calves sit up *front*. Besides, you don't know every cow on the island, smarty."

Everyone but Patty seemed to accept Chuck's story. Uncle Bo went back to rooting in his cornbread. Papa nodded politely before returning to his moospaper. Patty kept eyeing Dakota suspiciously, except when she would jump after getting poked by Mama's sewing needle.

"Sheldon, are you joining Chuck and Dakota for the contest today?" Mama asked. *Poke* went the needle. *Jump* went Patty.

"Um, yeah," Dakota answered shakily. "Yes, ma'am. Dakota's already at the beach. We're meeting him there." Hot tears welled up in his eyes. This was not what he had expected. Even *he* didn't recognize his own voice. There was no chance anyone would believe that he was actually Dakota. Not without having to hear an impossible story about magic shells and swirly genies. It was enough to break his heart.

"Haw! That's pretty spooky," Uncle Bo snorted, pointing a hoof at Chuck and "Sheldon." "You two look so much alike, maybe you ought to be brothers!"

"Humph," an unimpressed Patty huffed between pokes. "He's not even wearing a shirt."

✳ ✳ ✳

After "borrowing" a flowered red shirt from his own drawer, Dakota headed out with Chuck to Cape Cattle. The hot sun beat down on them as they hoofed across the island. As miserable as Dakota was about not being recognized, he was awfully glad to not be wearing his cowmouflage on such a blazing day.

Making their way across Bermooda Village, they saw Bullhorn Bay scattered with cows spending the hot Sunday enjoying the cool, calm water. Dakota wished he could feel as carefree as they looked. There were cows swimming, cows sailing, and cows standing on floating boards, paddling around with bamboo poles. The Porter calves trotted toward the cape, where they at last saw what they were looking for: cows surfing. They had finally reached the Cowabunga Classic.

Cape Cattle was a long spit of beach that stretched out into the Western Sea. On one side of the cape, big waves rolled offshore. On the other side, Cowabunga Falls rushed from the side of Mount Maverick in the distance. It was definitely the best spot on the island for a surf competition, especially one as big as the Cowabunga Classic.

Most of Bermooda had gathered to watch the contest. Everyone was sitting under colorful umbrellas that dotted the beach like drops of candy. In the middle of the herd, DJ Angus Atkins was setting up equipment on a platform. Angus had come down from his radio station atop the mountain to broadcast the contest on WKUD.

Dakota's new tail twitched and swished with excitement. Moving through the swarm of umbrellas, he was sure that someone here would know him. Chuck and Dakota waded through a sea of familiar faces. There were calves from school, cows from the village, creatures from all over the island…but none of them recognized the little brown cow walking beside Chuck. They asked questions much like the ones Patty had asked at the Porter House:

"Hey, who's the new calf?"

"Where's Dakota? Is he sick?"

"Isn't your brother usually with you?"

The afternoon heat was not making Dakota's stomachache feel any better, and the questions just made him feel even worse.

"All I wanted was to fit in," Dakota grumbled. "Now I do. So why am I in such an awful mooooood?" He covered his mouth with a hoof, surprised at how naturally the moo had come out.

"Maybe you were better off being yourself," Chuck suggested.

"Myself in *disguise*!" Dakota argued.

"It was still better than being a stranger, wasn't it?" Chuck said.

Dakota grimaced at the twisted purple shell in Chuck's hooves. "I can't believe you brought that thing with you."

"I didn't want Patty to find it. She's so nosy." Chuck peered into the shell as they walked. "I wonder what I should wish for."

"Careful, these wishes aren't all they're cracked up to be," Dakota warned.

"Oh, hush," Chuck snapped. "You got your wish. Now it's my turn. Should I wish to be as rich as the Wellingtons? Or maybe as smart as Cornelius?"

"*Maybe* we should go back to the Hortica Center and take another look at that book," Dakota cut in. "*Maybe* it can tell us something we might need to know."

"Now?" Chuck asked. "The contest is about to start! Besides, what more do we need to know?" He waved the shell back and forth. "*Unlimited wishes*, remember?"

"Put that thing away!" Dakota pleaded. "What if someone sees it? What if—"

Bump! Dakota was so busy bellyaching that he bounced right into the back end of an enormous bull pushing a heavy cart.

"Whoooa!" the bull mooed as he turned around. "*Lo'hai* there, little brother!"

Dakota had run into Leatherneck—a big, round globe of a bull with massive sloping shoulders and a belly that stuck out like a beach ball. Dark gray fur covered him everywhere but his nose, which was jet-black and had a heavy gold ring dangling from it. A shiny gold chain was draped around his thick nck, and the letter *L* was branded like a tattoo on each of his arms.

Anyone who didn't know Leatherneck might have been nervous bumping into such a character. But even though he looked tough, Leatherneck was a softie on the inside. His booming voice was friendly and jolly, and he was known to let calves crawl onto his hulking shoulders or hang from his curved horns. Wearing his bright red shirt with giant white flowers, Leatherneck reminded Dakota of a tropical Santa Claus…with cow horns.

"*Lo'hai*, Leatherneck!" Chuck piped up, tucking the shell under his shirt. "What's with the cart?"

Leatherneck was usually working at his cowfé on the edge of the village. But today, he was pushing around an oversize cart covered by a grassy canopy. The cart bumped and wobbled as it plowed over the sandy beach, with a cold cloud of icy air puffing from the boxes on its sides. A serving bar stretched across the front,

along with a big sign that read: *The Sandbar*.

"It's my new thing!" Leatherneck beamed proudly. "Frozen fruit! I got Chilly Cherries, Frosty Figs, Polar Pineapples…"

"Frozen?" Chuck asked. "Like with *ice*?" Ice was rare on a sunny tropical island. It was difficult to make, and even more difficult to keep.

"Sure, with ice!" Leatherneck grinned. He pointed to the cart. "But it melts pretty fast. So instead of making everyone come to my place, I bring my place to you! Hey, what do you two say to some Brisk Banana Blast? Perfect thing for a hot day!"

"Oog," the calves both mumbled. They'd had enough bananas during last night's feast.

"No bananas today, huh?" Leatherneck's ears drooped with disappointment. "Too bad your brother Dakota's not here. He'd love these things. Say, where is that little one, anyway?"

Dakota just slumped his shoulders and shook his head.

7
COW-A-BUNGA

The conversation with Leatherneck was cut short by a sudden shout from the crowd: "Look! There's Wahu!"

Everyone's heads turned toward a little shack about a hundred feet away. It wasn't much more than a small wooden box with a straw roof and a window facing the ocean. It stood right on the beach, atop four short stilts that lifted it only a few feet off the shore. A clothesline stretched from one corner of the shack's roof to a small shed nearby, and an array of surfboards stuck in the sand between the two. Clomping down the three small steps leading from the door was none other than Wahu Brahman.

Wahu was big, but not in the same way as Leatherneck. He was just as broad, but his shoulders were square, his belly was trim, and his chest was shaped like a barrel. Standing at seven feet tall, he filled the door as he stepped through. He was covered in fur just as blue as the ocean itself, and he wore a bright orange pair of Bermooda shorts.

It might have seemed strange that a bull as large as Wahu would live in so small a shack, but it fit his personality. Despite how admired he was, Wahu remaincd quite humble and preferred to live a simple life. Strolling from his beach box, he picked out a longboard from the collection outside. Wahu made all his own surfboards. Boardmaking was a Brahman family tradition that they had perfected through generations. Not only did every calf wish they could surf like Wahu Brahman, every calf wished they could have a Brahman board.

"All right, hooves and heifers," Angus Atkins blared into his microphone. "It's time for the fifty-seventh annual Cowabunga Classic! It's gonna be heavy! It's gonna be hairy! It's gonna be…*legen-dairy*!"

The surfers were all finished waxing their boards, and soon the contest was underway. There were nearly two dozen competitors, but the waves were cranking hard and many of them washed up pretty fast. The first to go was Barney Lineback. He was a clumsy bull who tumbled off his board, getting sucked up and pitched over by his very first wave.

"Ohhh! Barney goes over the falls and eats the surf!" Angus called out in his raspy voice. "Better luck next time, dude!"

Then came the Barzona twins, Dane and Devon. They tried to score points by matching each other's tricks, but they crashed into each other and wiped out at the exact same time.

"Yikes! Double dinged!" Angus bellowed. "Hang loose, guys."

An older gray bull named Choka Hanu hung in the contest for a long while until he "pearled" his board by accidentally pushing the nose underwater, ending his ride. Also eliminated were five of his students from the Choka Surf Acowdemy. One by one, surfcows wiped out and ate foam until there were only three competitors left.

The first finalist was Ivory Gelbray, a sturdy white hcifer riding the brightest yellow board anyone had ever seen. Dakota couldn't help thinking it looked like one of the magical bananas. The second finalist was Chopper Bullock, an intense young bull with fiery orange fur and an aggressive personality to match. He had already locked horns with a few other surfers that day. The third finalist was, of course, the strong and silent Wahu Brahman. The three of them floated on their boards, waiting for the wave that would roll them into victory.

Ivory watched the water rise. It wasn't the strongest-looking wave, but she didn't want to wait for a better one. She decided to take it.

"I've got this one, guys," she called out cheerily as she paddled into the wave earnestly. She popped up onto her board and started out with great form, turning up and down the face of the wave. But the wave, which hadn't looked very big to start, suddenly surged in size when passing over a shoal.

"Uh-oh," Angus announced. "Ivory's wave jacks up! This is a dangerous spot, folks. Let's see how she handles it!"

The rough wave began to curl fiercely, sending its heavy lip crashing toward Ivory's head. In a flash, she did the only smart thing she could do. She jumped off her board into the water to keep from getting crushed.

"No whey!" Angus shouted. "Ivory Gelbray bails to keep from getting axed! What a tough break for such a great surfer."

The wave washed over Ivory's head. She avoided getting pummeled, but her chances of winning were over. She paddled sadly to the shore, disappointed at her loss. There weren't a lot of heifer surfcows, so Ivory felt like she had something to prove.

"Aww," Chuck mooed. "That really is a shame."

"Good on you, Ivory," Angus consoled her as she trudged onto the beach. "Live to surf another day."

Wahu and Chopper remained in the water as it rose again. Wahu was a natural at knowing which swells were going to make the best waves, and he could tell this was going to be a big one. Maybe even a huge one. He plunged his arms in the water and started paddling. Chopper, who was determined to win, noticed Wahu going for it. He didn't feel like letting

Wahu have what might be the best wave of the day. As Wahu paddled to catch his wave, Chopper paddled right up behind him.

"This one's mine!" Chopper sneered, cutting between Wahu and the wave as it began to crest.

"Hey!" Dakota shouted. "He's snaking Wahu! He can't do that!" Dakota had been on Bermooda long enough to learn a bit about surfing. He knew that "snaking" was when one surfer sneaked behind another surfer to steal their wave. It wasn't against the rules. But it was a rotten thing to do.

Chopper showed off right away. He carved and shredded the crest of the wave, sending foam spray everywhere. It did look awfully impressive.

"That's Chopper Bullock with some wicked slashing!" announced Angus. "Strong start from the young challenger!"

Wahu didn't seem bothered. He just kept his eyes forward as he dropped down the face of the wave. He pumped for speed, reaching down and grabbing the sides of his board as he glided along. Then he stepped to the front of his board, hanging the four points of his hooves over the nose and arching his back.

"Wahu Brahman hangs four and pulls off a sweet soul arch!" Angus called from the beach. "Nice move by the champ!"

The wave rose higher and higher. Wahu and Chopper kept charging down the ever-growing face of the wave.

"Sixty feet! Seventy feet! Eighty feet!" Angus shouted as the wave rose higher. "This...is...*epic!*"

"Wow!" Dakota's eyes opened wide. "How tall is that wave gonna go?"

At ninety feet, the top of the wave finally tumbled down, creating a perfect tube for the surfcows to barrel through. Wahu stuck out his hoof and drew a line in the face of the wave as both surfers vanished inside its green tunnel.

Chopper took that moment to make his move. He taunted Wahu by riding up onto the back of his board.

"Come on, Brahman—moooove it!" he teased. "This ain't no party wave, champ!"

Chopper's surfboard—which was shaped like one of the crocodile's teeth that hung on his necklace—had a little set of bullhorns attached to the nose that he kept trying to hook the tail of Wahu's board with. But Chopper started having just a little too much fun. As they came out of the tube in a spray of foam, the whole crowd on the beach could see him trying to throw Wahu off.

"Hey!" Chuck bellowed. "He can't do that!"

Wahu made trick cuts back and forth with his board, trying to shake Chopper off. Finally, Wahu ran up the side of the wave and launched himself into the air. His board spun around in a complete circle as he switched his stance, putting his right hoof forward instead of his left. As he came down, he landed on the board facing the opposite direction.

"Amoozing!" Angus cheered. "Wahu Brahman switches midair to Goofy Hoof with an awesome three-sixty alley-oop!"

"Moo-hoooooooo!" Chuck and Dakota cheered from the beach along with the rest of the crowd.

Meanwhile, Chopper had been so busy with his bully-boarding that he got completely shacked by the monstrous wave. The crashing surf drove him underwater, snapping the leash that attached his surfboard to his leg.

Wahu, now facing the beach, saw Chopper go under. He jumped off his board, pulled off his own leash, and dove underwater. A few seconds later, two surfers appeared on the surface—a blue one helping along an orange one.

Their ride was officially over. Wahu dragged Chopper to the shore, both of their boards lost in the sea. Chopper had done a lot of showing off, but Wahu had gone the distance and had a better run. And as Wahu pulled the coughing, sputtering Chopper out of the froth, it was pretty clear who the winner was.

8

THE CHAMP

"Easy, brah," Wahu said in his deep voice as he helped Chopper ashore. "Just take it easy."

"Back off, cheater!" Chopper roared, shaking off Wahu's helpful hooves. He stomped up to Angus and the contest judges. "Did you see that? He dropped in on me! He cut right in front of me and totally spoiled my ride!"

"Bull!" Dakota shouted from the crowd. "Everyone saw you snake Wahu! You tried to steal his wave!"

"You were pretty aggressive," one of the judges said.

"Really, Chopper," Angus agreed. "Quit milking it, dude."

The crowd murmured in agreement. Chopper started to complain again, but it was no use. The whole accident had been his fault, and everyone knew it. The contest was over, and Chopper Bullock sulked off in defeat. Angus held up Wahu's arm with one hoof and handed him the Cowabunga Trophy with the other.

"The winner—and *still* champion—of the annual Cowabunga Classic...Wahuuuuuu

Brahmaaaaannn!" he announced. "Let's have a round of cowpplause for the Big Cowhuna!"

The beach erupted into a chorus of happy moos. Dakota still hadn't gotten used to the idea of mooing instead of clapping, but he joined in as usual. After all, cow hooves weren't the best for clapping.

"How about it, Wahu?" Angus asked the dripping-wet champ. "That was one gnarly battle of cattle. Why'd you cut your ride short for the dude who snaked you?"

"You always help out another surfer in danger, brah," Wahu's voice boomed into the microphone. "No matter what, no matter who. I'd do the same for any of you. You should do the same for one another."

The excited moos continued.

"*Moohalo*." Wahu thanked his fans with a polite wave before leaving the crowd and quietly heading toward his shack, holding his new trophy.

"Wow, he sure didn't stick around long," Dakota said.

"He never does, little bro," Angus said. "That dude never hangs around for the cowpplause. He just loves the thrill of the ride. *That's* what makes him a champ."

Chuck, who had been unusually quiet, watched as Wahu disappeared into his shack. He spied the small shed that stood across from the shack. *I'll bet he keeps his best boards in there*, Chuck thought. He turned his attention to the collection of surfboards plunked in the sand outside, all of which sported the Brahman logo. They weren't fancy or flashy. But they were smooth, polished, and perfect.

"Uncle Bo is wrong," Chuck mumbled. "I bet I could be as good a surfer as Wahu, if only I had a Brahman board."

"If only you had a board at all," Dakota pointed out, remembering the broken surfboard in Chuck's closet.

Chuck's tail began twitching and swishing. "Ooh! Ooh!" he mooed. "I have an idea!" Dodging into some tall beach grass nearby, he

pulled the shell out and knocked a hoof on it three times. *Clang, clang, clang!*

"Helloooooo, Zephyrrrrr," he called.

The cloudy genie slowly slithered out of his shell. "Good day, sir." He yawned as though he had just woken from a nap. "I trust your wishes are—"

"Yeah, yeah—good day," Chuck interrupted. "Zephyr, I know what I want to wish for!"

"I'm overjoyed, sir," Zephyr said flatly. "Your wish is always my command."

Dakota thought Zephyr sounded a lot more annoyed than overjoyed. Perhaps he didn't like being interrupted.

Chuck pointed toward Wahu's shack. "Zephyr, I wish to have a Brahman board," he said. "No, wait—*lots* of Brahman boards! *And*…I wish to be a champion surfer! Just like Wahu Brahman!"

Dakota thought Chuck was overdoing things a bit, but it was too late to protest.

"As you wish," came Zephyr's usual reply.

The familiar whipping of wind began as Zephyr worked his magic. Grains from the beach stung their eyes and gritted in their teeth as a tiny sandstorm circled them.

Once everything settled, Chuck and Dakota wiped the sand from their eyes and looked around. They were not standing on the beach anymore, but on a bamboo mat in a small but cozy bedroom. The walls and floor were made of weathered old wood, and a thatched roof of thickly woven beach grass was over their heads. A canvas hammock was stretched across the middle of the room. In one corner was a stool with a quilted blanket folded on it. In the opposite corner was a box full of trophies covered in dust, except for a new one that sat on a small table to their right. Against the wall in front of them was a small dresser with a grimy mirror above it. The soft sound of the ocean rolled in through the window. Chuck wasn't sure where they were, but he knew one thing for certain: he was soaked to the bone.

"Where are we?" Chuck asked. "When did I get so wet?" He looked down at Dakota. "And when did you get so small?"

Dakota gazed up at Chuck but couldn't manage any words. All his open jaw could do was sputter out: "Hububbubba..."

Chuck spotted the trophy on the table. "Whoa!" he mooed, picking it up. "Are we inside Wahu's shack?"

"Hububbubba..." Dakota repeated, pointing at the mirror.

"What is it?" Chuck looked in the smudgy mirror. But the reflection he saw didn't look like himself. He blinked a few times and took a closer look. No, he *definitely* didn't look like Chuck.

He was huge.

He was blue.

He was Wahu Brahman.

THE REAL WAHU

Chuck panicked at the reflection in the mirror. He dropped the trophy and the shell, both clattering to the floor. His eyes went wide as coconuts as he let out a long and loud moo.

"What did you do?" he bellowed at Zephyr with his nostrils flared. "I wished to be *like* Wahu Brahman. I didn't say I wanted to *be* Wahu Brahman! What am I supposed to do now?"

"My sincere apologies, sir," Zephyr droned. "I thought this would be the best way to make you just like the one you think so highly of. And I must say, you look quite impressive."

"Relax—it's no big deal," Dakota said, picking up the shell. "All you have to do is just wish to be yourself again."

"Oh. Right," Chuck said, calming down a little. He took a deep breath and looked in the mirror again, this time with less panic. He couldn't help but agree with Zephyr. He did look impressive. Chuck never was the biggest or toughest calf on the island. But now he wasn't Chuck anymore. Now he was…*Wahu Brahman*. He was strong and massive. He was the Big Cowhuna. He raised his brow over one eye and flexed his giant arms in the mirror.

"Chuck!" Dakota snapped. "You should wish yourself back!"

"Oh…um…yeah," Chuck agreed. "Yeah, I

know. Okay." But before he could say another word, there was a sudden knock at the door of the shack.

"Who's that?" Dakota asked, jerking his head around. "Are you expecting company?"

"How can I be expecting company?" Chuck asked. "I'm not even *me*!"

Dakota pulled the quilted blanket from the hammock and fanned Zephyr toward the shell. "Quick, Zephyr! Hide!"

"As you wish, sir," Zephyr said, quietly shrinking back into the shell with a gentle hiss.

Dakota covered Zephyr's shell with the quilt. He stuffed it under the stool as Chuck opened the door. Outside they found nearly every calf they knew from school mobbed around Wahu's beach box. They all excitedly chattered at once:

"Wow, Wahu! That was a-moo-zing!"

"Would you teach me how to surf like that?"

"Can I have your autograph?"

Chuck felt very overwhelmed by the stampede of attention. He knew he didn't deserve any of it. After all, it wasn't really *him* who won had the Cowabunga Classic. "No, no…really," he said in Wahu's deep voice, holding up an enormous set of hooves. "It was no big deal."

Chuck's modesty was met with a throng of protests from the starstruck calves:

"What do you mean?"

"Of course it's a big deal!"

"Wahu, you're the greatest!"

Chuck froze. No one had ever called him the greatest before. Usually he was the weirdo cow who didn't fit in and didn't have a lot of friends. Now he was suddenly "the greatest"? He looked down at all the calves. They were all so much smaller than him now. They seemed so far beneath him. Chuck had been an outsider for so long…what was wrong with finally being everyone's hero for a change?

"You're right." He nodded to the crowd as a smirk grew across his snout. "I *am* the greatest."

Dakota saw the gleam of pride burning in Chuck's eyes as he signed autographs. Dakota knew right then that Chuck would not be wishing himself back anytime soon.

✹ ✹ ✹

That night, Chuck and Dakota built a small campfire on the beach outside Wahu's shack. There they sat, bathed in flickering orange firelight that sent shadows dancing all over the sand. Around them were piles of more and more chocolate-covered bananas. Chuck was a full-sized bull now, so he figured he could eat more bananas without getting sick like last time. He stuffed his face full as he polished the dusty trophies from Wahu's shack. The warm light from the fire flashed across the line of Brahman surfboards stuck in the sand next to the shack. *They're all* my *boards now*, Chuck thought to himself.

"I wonder why Wahu had all these trophies sitting in a box," Chuck wondered aloud.

"Maybe he didn't care so much about the trophies," Dakota offered. "Like Angus said. He just loved the thrill of the ride."

He thought about how these wishes kept bringing unexpected results. "Have you noticed that every time we wish for something we want, it also comes with something we *don't* want?" he noted. "We wished for tons of chocolate bananas and we ended up with stomachaches. I wished to be a real cow, and now no one recognizes me. It's like every wish has a downside."

"Downside? What downside?" Chuck asked, munching on a banana. "I'm *Wahu Brahman*, for mooing out loud. The greatest surfcow who ever rode a board. And you? You never have to hide behind a costume again. So where's the downside?"

Dakota didn't answer. He could see that arguing would be difficult when Chuck was so pleased with himself. "Where do you suppose the *real* Wahu is?" he asked instead.

"I *am* the real Wahu," Chuck answered, pounding his oversized chest. He tugged on a tuft of his new blue hair. "See? This is real."

Dakota was becoming annoyed. "Are you going to wish yourself back or not?"

"I don't know." Chuck shrugged, admiring his huge new arms. "Maybe. Probably. But not yet."

"What are you going to do about school tomorrow?" Dakota asked.

"Nothing." Chuck laughed as he gobbled down another banana. "The Big Cowhuna doesn't go to school."

Dakota wished Chuck would take this a little more seriously. But Chuck was really enjoying all the attention he was getting as Wahu.

"What are *you* going to do about school?" Chuck asked him back, wiping chocolate from his big blue mouth.

Dakota hadn't thought about that. It was obvious that none of the calves had recognized him on the beach that day. He couldn't go to school like this, and he certainly couldn't go back to the Porter House. He took a chocolate-covered bite of banana, but he didn't enjoy the sweet taste anymore. Every delicious morsel just reminded him of how he was, once again, without a home. Gazing into the campfire, he began to wonder if he should wish to be hu'man again. But he had wanted for so long to walk around without wearing cowmouflage. Was he really ready to give that up now? The more he thought about it, the more his head began to hurt the same way his stomach had that morning.

"I'm going to sleep," he told Chuck, climbing the three small steps to Wahu's door. "Maybe everything will make more sense in the morning."

THE SEARCH PARTY

The next morning, Chuck and Dakota awoke to a familiar voice calling both of their names.

"Chuuuuuuuck! Dakooooooota!"

They rushed outside and found Patty Porter patrolling the beach with her hooves cupped to her mouth, calling their names over and over again. She spied Dakota right away, recognizing the odd calf who had showed up at the Porter House the day before.

"Hey, you! Sheldon!" she called, huffing up to them. "Have you seen them?"

"What's going on?" Chuck asked.

"We're looking for my brothers, Chuck and Dakota Porter," Patty babbled. "They didn't come home last night. They didn't show up at school this morning either. The whole island is looking for them."

Chuck and Dakota saw dozens of familiar Bermoodans combing the beach. Cornelius, Leatherneck, Angus…Even Chopper Bullock, who left yesterday's contest in disgrace, was helping the search.

"Last anyone knows, they were with

III

Sheldon here at the Cowabunga Classic," Patty went on, pointing to Dakota.

"I honestly haven't seen them since yesterday," Dakota said. That wasn't a total lie since they'd both been in different bodies then.

"Will you help us look for them, Wahu?" Patty pleaded. "Chuck looks a lot like Sheldon here, except he's white with brown spots. Dakota is brown with blue eyes, and he looks kind of…well…lumpy and tattered."

"Of course," Chuck said. "I'm the 'Big Cowhuna.' What kind of local hero would I be if I didn't offer my help?"

Dakota fumed and rolled his eyes. Real heroes didn't *call* themselves heroes. He glanced past Patty and saw Mama Porter pacing circles in the beach grass, wringing her hooves and looking more frantic than he'd ever seen her. Tears of worry rolled from her normally cheerful eyes. Dakota grabbed the edge of Chuck's orange shorts and pulled him behind the shack.

"Okay, this has gone on long enough," he said, craning his neck up. "We *have* to wish ourselves back."

"But I'm not ready to go back!" Chuck whined, which sounded funny in Wahu's deep voice. "I haven't gotten to ride any of my boards yet. Or finish polishing my trophies!"

"They're not yours!" Dakota scolded. "You didn't *work* for any of that! You just *wished* for it!"

"Oh yeah?" Chuck said. "Well…you didn't work to be a real cow either!" Chuck knew that made no sense, but he was running out of arguments.

"You're crazy!" Dakota yelped. He reached for the shell. "That's it. I'm wishing us back."

"Oh, no you're not," Chuck said, holding the shell high over Dakota's head. Dakota jumped up and down, swiping and grabbing at the shell dangling just out of reach. But it was no use.

"Look, you're not Wahu," Dakota said. "You're nothing like him. He didn't love attention like this."

Chuck's face drooped a little. He wondered if he was enjoying the fame to much.

"Do you think Mama wants *Wahu* to come home?" Dakota continued. "Think about how much it would take to feed you! Mama deserves to have the *real* Chuck at home."

Chuck scratched his head with an enormous hoof. All he had wanted was to be popular and talented. He hadn't thought about what it took to get that stuff. And he certainly hadn't wanted to hurt anyone, especially not his own mama.

For a minute, Dakota thought he was finally getting through. But then he saw Chuck's new blue tail twitching furiously.

"I have an idea! She *can* have the real Chuck at home!" Chuck squinted into the distance, like he was looking for something.

"Remember last night when you asked where the real Wahu is? Well, if I'm in Wahu's body, he must be out there in *mine* somewhere!" He knocked on the shell. "Psst! Hey, Zephyr!"

Zephyr breezed out from the shell. "Good morning, sir. I almost didn't recognize you."

"No one does," Chuck said. "They're all looking for us. So I wish for Wahu—Chuck—*whatever*…to show up here. *Right now*."

Dakota thought this was Chuck's worst idea ever. But Zephyr was happy to help.

"As you wish, sir," he said.

A sandy cloud swirled up from the beach just a stone's throw away from the shack. Out of the cloud stumbled Chuck—rather, Wahu in Chuck's body—with a puzzled look on his face. He appeared to have wandered the island all night.

"See?" Chuck said. "There he is! Now, when we 'find' him, Mama will be happy and we'll be heroes! We can have our bananas and eat them too!"

Dakota hated this plan. He wondered if Chuck's brain had not come along when he got swooshed into Wahu's body. As it turned out, they didn't have to find the little calf—he found them. Wahu spotted his own big blue body just as Zephyr disappeared inside his shell.

"Hey!" Little-Wahu cried out in Chuck's tiny voice. "Hey, brah! What are you doing in my skin?" He stormed over to them, a very big bull in a very small body.

"Hey, relax." Big-Chuck put his hooves up. "It's cool."

"It's not cool, brah!" Little-Wahu yelled. "Get out of there! Give me back my body!"

"Shh! Calm down!" Big-Chuck said. He dropped the shell to the ground, put his hooves under the little calf's arms, and picked him up to eye level.

"Hey! Hooves off, brah! Put me down!" Wahu, who was always so calm and cool, was now throwing a world-class fit. He carried on so loudly that Patty overheard.

"Look! It's Chuck!" Patty shouted. Everyone searching the area turned and looked. But instead of seeing a missing calf being rescued, they saw him kicking and

screaming and thrashing in a big bull's arms while hollering, "Let me go! Give me back my body!"

"Uh-oh," Big-Chuck muttered. This was not the outcome he had hoped for.

"There you are!" Mama said as they rushed to the shack. She scooped up Little-Wahu from Big-Chuck's arms and kissed him on the head.

"Wait a minute," Little-Wahu said. "Who are you?"

Mama looked shocked and even more heartbroken than before.

"What's going on here?" Papa Porter demanded.

"What did you do to him?" Patty asked. "Why doesn't he remember us?"

"This poser stole my body!" Little-Wahu screeched. "He's not the Big Cowhuna!"

Now, the talking cows of Bermooda may have been remarkable, but they were still cows...and cows get spooked easily. The search party began to whisper and wonder. Was there more to Wahu than they knew?

"See?" Chopper Bullock said. "I *told* you this blue galoot can't be trusted!"

More and more folks joined the crowd. The very same cows who had praised Wahu yesterday now surrounded him, filled with suspicion. As the thickening mob started to raise tough questions, Dakota slipped away and crept under Wahu's shack with the magic shell.

There wasn't much room under the shack. Hunched over in the sand with Wahu's floor just above his head, Dakota knocked on the shell three times: *Clank...clank...clank!*

Zephyr slithered out of his shell into the tight space. His cloud coiled like a snake around Dakota, who crouched down on his hooves.

"Zephyr, things are getting out of control here," Dakota whispered into the surrounding cloud, not sure where to look while he was speaking.

"It certainly looks that way," Zephyr replied. "But I must ask, sir, is life ever *really* in control?"

"Maybe not," Dakota uttered. "But it

sure seems like these wishes have some drawbacks."

"Well, things rarely come free, sir," Zephyr chuckled. That chuckle bothered Dakota. Was Zephyr enjoying this mess? The crowd outside grew louder and more heated.

"Listen, we just need everyone to chill out so I can figure out what to do next," Dakota said.

"Gladly, sir," Zephyr agreed. "Would you kindly make that an official wish?"

"Fine, whatever!" Dakota snapped. "*I wish* for everything to just...*cool down.*"

Zephyr's magical wind went to work. "As you wish, *sir*," he crooned.

Dakota didn't like the way Zephyr had said *sir*. It sounded like he knew something Dakota didn't. But his thoughts were soon shattered by a shriek: "What is *that*?!"

Dakota scooped up the shell as Zephyr poofed back inside. Scurrying out from under the shack, he looked around and saw exactly what was causing such a panic. The air had suddenly gotten much colder, and the sky—which normally burned bright blue—was now full of frozen white flakes that fell from the clouds.

"Impossible!" Dakota whispered.

Bermooda, the warm and sunny tropical island, was being covered in snow.

11

SNOW PROBLEM

Snowflakes twinkled as they fluttered onto the beach, making the sand dunes sparkle like diamonds. The oleander bushes shimmered as cold white fluff piled up on their hot pink flowers. The palm trees were all capped with stacks of snow as though the trees were wearing soft white hats. It actually looked rather pretty. It reminded Dakota of a tropical snow globe, where a palm tree on a tiny plastic island would be flooded with impossible snowflakes that could never actually happen.

But cows, as you know, get spooked easily. They didn't appreciate the beauty of Bermooda's first snowfall. Instead, they panicked.

"What is it?"

"It's cold!"

"It stings! It stings! Owowowowow!"

"It's okay!" Dakota assured them, stashing the shell in his shirt pocket. "It's just snow."

"Snow?" Patty squealed as she shivered. "What's snow?"

"It's like tiny ice falling from the sky." Dakota held out his hoof to catch the flakes.

"It's fun. You can throw snowballs, make a snow fort, build a snowmaer, snow*cow*..."

"Ice?" Leatherneck interrupted. His face, which usually sported a wide smile, was drawn into a frown. "That's impossible! Do you know how hard it is to make ice? That kinda stuff don't just fall out of the sky!"

Chopper Bullock suddenly recognized Dakota as the little brown calf who had embarrassed him at the Cowabunga Classic. "Wait a minute," he sneered. "How do you know so much about this 'snow'?"

"Who are you, anyway?" Patty chimed in. "I asked around yesterday about a brown calf named Sheldon, and no one's ever even heard of you!"

It was now Dakota's turn to face the mob. They fired a flurry of questions at him, not giving him a chance to answer any of them:

"Where did you come from?"

"Who is your kine?"

"Why hasn't anyone seen you before?"

"This all started when you showed up

yesterday!" Patty accused him. "First Dakota disappeared, then Chuck disappeared, and now this crazy snow! You brought this on us! Make it go away!"

Trembling in the cold, the anxious crowd mooed in agreement.

"You don't understand," Big-Chuck stepped in. "It's not his fault. See, there's this magic shell…"

"Magic shell?" Leatherneck repeated.

"Is he serious?" Patty cried.

"They've *both* gone mad!" Chopper boomed. "Mad cows!"

The crowd went from frightened to angry. They stamped their hooves and snorted. Dakota may not have grown up on Bermooda, but he knew what to do when facing a mob of angry cattle. He suddenly wished he wasn't wearing a red shirt.

"Run!" Dakota shouted.

Chuck and Dakota ran. The horde of spooked cattle charged after them. They rushed toward the trees, hoping to lose the stampede in Bermooda's thick jungle. Dakota tried to scramble up the closest banana tree, but his hooves just slipped and slid on the smooth tree trunk. In a flash, he remembered he no longer had the hu'man fingers and toes that made climbing trees so easy. He was a real calf now, and, after all, he had wished to never have to climb a banana tree again.

They both ran deeper into the snowy jungle, with Chuck in the lead and Dakota falling behind. By the time Dakota reached the hilly base of Lookout Bluff, he had lost sight of Chuck completely. He stood on an icy mound, frantically looking for a place to hide as the crowd got closer. Suddenly a big blue arm reached up, grabbed his leg, and pulled him down off the hill. Chuck had found a tiny hollow space under the knoll. They kept their heads down and their mouths shut until the angry crowd had gone past and all was quiet.

"I think we lost them," Chuck said. They now heard nothing but tiny ringing laughter. Laughter coming from Dakota's shirt pocket. Dakota pulled the shell from his pocket and put it to his ear. Sure enough, the sound of giggling had replaced the sound of the ocean.

"Hey!" Dakota snarled in a hushed whisper and he knocked on the shell. "Zephyr! Swirl yourself out here *now*!"

Zephyr obediently swirled out of his shell. Indeed, he was snickering at the whole situation. "Is everything 'cooled down' enough for you, sir?" he asked between chuckles.

"You think this is *funny*?" Dakota asked. "I didn't wish for snow! Why would you do this?"

"Why?" Zephyr repeated. "Why? Because *I'm bored*, that's why! Do you know what it's like giving everyone whatever they want all day, every day, for thousands of years? It's even more boring than sitting inside that shell! Why shouldn't I mix it up with a little fun for myself?" Zephyr's cloud grew darker and lightning flashed inside.

"And believe me—this is *very* fun!" he continued, his voice getting deeper. "You'd be surprised how greedy one can be when one has unlimited wishes. No matter what happens, folks just *can't…quit…wishing!*"

"Make all this stop!" Chuck demanded.

Zephyr spun a little faster. "Is that your wish…*sir?* Think carefully!"

Chuck and Dakota stiffened. Zephyr was clearly waiting to have fun with another one of their wishes. What if he decided to stop time completely? Or something even worse?

"See? You don't have the power to beat me!" the mischievous genie screeched. "The only way to stop me is to stop wishing! Do you have the power to stop wishing, you greedy little cows?" Zephyr's laughter grew harder and louder. So hard that tears fell from his cloudy eyes like raindrops. So loud that it echoed off the rocks like thunder.

"There they are!" came Chopper's voice from the trees. Chuck and Dakota poked their heads up to see the bright orange bull running toward them, followed by what appeared to be most of Bermooda slushing through the deepening snow. Zephyr had spoiled their hiding place. Chuck and Dakota charged up the cold slope of the bluff with the whole herd in hot pursuit.

Zephyr no longer hid from view. He hung out of his shell, trailing behind Dakota and cackling wildly as the snow fell down even heavier. "Waaaaaahuuuuuuuu!" Zephyr mockingly howled. "I'm the *Big Cowhuna!*"

"That twisted genie's gone crazy!" Dakota yelped. "He's completely bananas!"

No sooner had Dakota said the words than dozens of chocolate-covered bananas suddenly began popping up out of thin air. They rained down from the sky, slapping Chuck and Dakota in the face and falling under their feet as they ran. Chuck quickly started plucking bananas from the air,

opening them, and throwing the peels on the icy ground behind them. Chopper slipped on one of the peels and fell sprawling onto the ground, tripping up several other cows.

Dakota and Chuck continued all the way to the edge of the cliff, where Lookout Light stood covered in icicles.

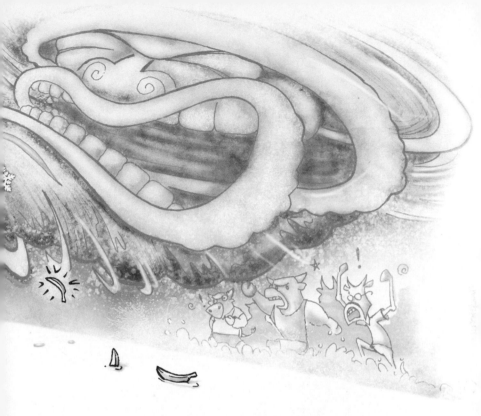

"Do something!" Chuck said as they scrambled up the lighthouse steps. "I'm all out of ideas!"

"What am I supposed to do?" Dakota cried over the sound of Zephyr's hysterical laughter. "Anything I wish for, this genie will just twist into a nightmare!" Bananas rained down on their heads. "Everything's completely messed up! All because of this stupid shell! *I wish we'd never even found this horrible thing!*"

Zephyr's laughter suddenly stopped. In fact, everything slowed down and stopped, as if time itself had become as frozen as the weather. Bermooda was blanketed in a thick silence, disturbed only by a slight whispering voice: *"As you wish."*

All at once, life began moving slowly in reverse. The snowflakes fell upward. The crowd ran backward down the bluff, followed by Chuck and Dakota. Bananas disappeared into thin air. Then things began moving faster and faster. The campfire, the surf contest, Leatherneck's cart…it all whipped past

Chuck and Dakota in a blur as they felt their bodies being pulled backward and memories being pulled from their heads. The blur became a white haze, and the haze became a bright flash. Before they knew it, there was nothing around them but a brilliant light and the peaceful sound of the ocean.

12

DÉJÀ MOO

Chuck and Dakota lounged in the thick grass under the tall banana trees. The day was quiet and peaceful. No mysteries, no discoveries, no adventures of any kind. Just the crashing of waves, a warm breeze, and the gentle cawing of seagulls. As far as Dakota was concerned, it was perfect.

"Pass me another banana," he said.

"This is the last one," Chuck said, tossing it to him. "If you want more, you'll have to climb another tree."

Dakota looked up at the trees towering over them. He felt quite relaxed at the moment and was not in the mood to scramble back up and fetch any more bananas. Propping his back against a tree, he pulled his straw hat down over his eyes and folded his hands behind his head.

Meanwhile Chuck paced back and forth in the grass. "I'm soooooo boooooored!" Chuck mooed. "Aren't you bored?"

"Nope," Dakota replied from under his hat. "I'm just fine right here."

But Dakota felt something peculiar about that question. *Did we have this discussion once before?* he thought. He heard the sound of Chuck clomping over to him. Suddenly his eyes were treated to a flood of warm sunlight as Chuck pulled the hat off his face.

"Can we at least take a walk?" Chuck asked.

As Dakota blinked in the sudden brightness, the odd feeling got stronger. Yes, he was *certain* they'd had this discussion once before. Dakota racked his brain as he climbed to his feet.

"Sure," he said, adjusting his cow mask.

They ambled toward the beach and strolled along the shore. But as they walked, Dakota still could not shake the strange sensation. Everything they did and every word they said felt so familiar, like an old recording that was being replayed or a chapter in some book he'd already read.

"Are you getting a weird feeling right now?" Dakota asked. "Like we've already done this? That we've had this exact same conversation?"

"You mean *déjà moo*?" Chuck asked. "It's when you feel like you've already grazed in a certain pasture once before."

"Whatever," Dakota said. "This whole thing just feels way too familiar."

"Of course it feels familiar," Chuck sighed, picking up a rock from the beach. "We've probably made this boring walk a billion times." He tossed the rock far ahead of them. It whizzed through the air and landed in the soft sand with a loud *clank!*

Chuck and Dakota exchanged confused looks.

"What was that clanking noise?" Chuck wondered aloud.

They trotted up to the place where the rock had landed, looking for the source of the sound. There, half-buried in the sand, they found a shiny purple shell.

The shell was twisted into a cone-shaped spiral like a tiny tornado. Its entire surface was covered with a pattern of loops and swirls, as if thousands of permanent fingerprints had been left all over it. A string of symbols was etched along its twisted spiral curve. They almost looked like letters but not in any language that Chuck or Dakota could read.

"Wow!" Chuck said. "Now *this* is amazing!" He turned the shell over in his hooves. "Look at these weird loopy patterns! And these markings! It almost looks like some kind of ancient writing. I've never seen anything like this before."

"Are you sure?" Dakota shivered as he looked down at the strange shell. "I don't know. I feel like I recognize it somehow."

Glowing in the late afternoon sun, the shell looked as though it were alive. A gleam ran across its pearly purple surface, as if it were telling Dakota that it knew something he didn't know.

Chuck shook his head. "Don't you get it?" he asked. "Nothing like this occurs in nature. *This shell shouldn't be here.*"

"Well, I can fix that," Dakota said. He snatched the shell out of Chuck's hooves and flung it as hard as he could out into the ocean. It disappeared beneath the churning surf with a tiny *ploop!*

"So long, weirdo shell!" Dakota called out into the rolling waves. "Best wishes! You don't belong here!"

"Heeeeeeyyy!" Chuck whined. "I was gonna keep that! You know I like to collect cool stuff!"

"Every time you find something weird, it always gets us into some kind of trouble," Dakota reminded him.

Disappointed, Chuck gazed at the spot where Dakota had thrown the shell. Beyond it, they saw Wahu Brahman surfing in the distance. Tomorrow, Wahu would be competing in the Cowabunga Classic, where dozens of calves would be following him with starry eyes. As they watched Wahu practice, Dakota tugged and pulled on his cowmouflage, which had started to itch in the warm sun.

"Boy, I'd sure love it if I didn't have to wear this costume anymore," Dakota muttered.

"Sorry," Chuck said. "I don't think Bermooda is ready for a hu'man just yet." He really did feel bad that Dakota had to stay in disguise all the time, but he knew that cows spook pretty easy. He changed the subject.

"Hey, you know what would taste good on those?" he said, pointing to the banana still in Dakota's hand. "Chocolate!"

"Ugh. No thanks," Dakota grimaced. For some reason, this delicious idea made him feel sick to his stomach. "Speaking of food, we should head home. It's almost suppertime. We don't want to be late."

Chuck agreed. They started off toward

the Porter House, but not before Chuck took one last look at the tiny blue shape of Wahu shredding waves out in the ocean.

"You know, I'll bet I get to be as good a surfer as Wahu Brahman someday," Chuck said.

"Ha," Dakota chuckled, finishing his banana. "You wish."

NOW iN PAPERBACK!

NOW iN PAPERBACK!

153